HELEN OF THE WEST

by Tre Chado

I0652951

Helen of the West: Bloodline of the Tide 1 is a lyrical journey through salt and sacrifice, where folklore meets faith and the sea remembers everything.

Helen is a woman haunted by love, loss, and a voice on the wind calling her home. When her husband and children vanish westward, she makes the unthinkable choice to follow, disguised, hunted, and ultimately transformed.

What begins as a search becomes a reckoning. As Helen faces storms both natural and supernatural, she must decide whether the tides will take her... or awaken her.

From the first whispered lullaby to the last gasp beneath the waves, *Helen of the West* is a testament to the memory of love, the rhythm of ancestral spirit, and the cost of walking toward the unknown.

COPYRIGHT

DEDICATION

For Chado West

CHAPTER LIST:

CHAPTER 1: HELEN

There she was, standing on the dock. The wind whispered secrets only she could hear, wrapping its fingers through her long black hair, shimmering like black ice beneath the fading light of dusk.

Her name was Helen.

Though the ocean had swallowed so much of her life, it had never taken her memories.

This wasn't her first time here.

She had walked these wooden planks as a girl, holding the rough, blistered hand of her father—a renowned rigger whose calloused palms were cracked like old leather, yet warm as the midday sun. The men respected him not for his strength, but for his silence. He was a man who spoke with knots and ropes, who read the sea like scripture.

Helen idolized him. She would mimic his hand movements, trace the thick scars across his knuckles, and boast to the village children,

"I have my daddy's hands."

One stormy evening, when the sea thrashed against the harbor and the sky split with violet lightning, she remembered standing beneath the overhang with him.

"Storms speak loud when hearts are too quiet," he had said. "You listen to the sea, Helen. It knows your name."

That night, he sang her an old sailor's chant, half lullaby, half warding prayer. She still hummed it when sleep wouldn't come.

But her father died young—too young. They said it was sickness. Others said the witch cursed him for refusing her a favor. Some whispered he had crossed a line with the spirits, tied the wrong knot during a blood moon voyage. Superstition ran through the village like a current through open water, and Helen, though skeptical, couldn't ignore the timing. His last breath came during the waning phase of a red moon.

Now she stood where they had once stood, but this time she was alone.

The scent of sea salt and tar filled her nose. Gulls cried out in the distance. Behind her, the sounds of the village began to quiet as lamps were lit and doors were bolted shut. But she remained still, her eyes fixed westward, beyond the horizon, where the sky bled into water like bruised silk.

She wasn't here for memory. She was here for Saint—her husband.

He had gone west two grueling years ago on a voyage to find work and stability for their family. The last time she saw him, he had stood right here, his arms full of rope and determination.

He kissed her like it would be the last time, though he promised otherwise.

They had met at the beach, just beyond the ridge of the cove. She was barefoot, dancing with the wind. He was watching from a boat that hadn't yet docked. Their eyes met across the surf—not romantic, not naive. It was a knowing. No butterflies, no bubbles. Just silence and trust. A look that said,

"I see the ache in you. I've carried it too."

Their love wasn't loud. It was built through stillness—stargazing in hammocks, long talks by candlelight, and gentle touches while their children slept.

They married in the rigger's yard beneath the gaze of the full moon. Her father had passed away by then, but she wore one of his ropes around her waist, braided three times, symbolic of lineage, love, and labor.

They had four children. Three followed Saint when he left. She kept the oldest, Grace, whose spirit reminded her too much of herself. Saint said it would be safer if he took the younger ones. Less chance they'd be taken by the wrong hands in the west. Less trauma.

The parting had felt like a splitting of her soul. That night, she sat on the dock for hours, clutching a candle that would not stay lit.

She hadn't received a letter in nearly seven months.

The last one had been simple.

"We're alive. Light is learning to tie knots. Tempest sings like you. Storm asks about your bread. Soon, Helen. Soon."

Soon had become never.

Her neighbors began to murmur. The healer with the bone charms said her spirit was thinning. The butcher's wife said she looked like a shadow trying to walk as flesh. But Helen didn't care.

Something was pulling her—not just love, but an ancestral tide she couldn't name. Her dreams had changed. She saw her father standing in a boat made of teeth, waving toward a storm. She saw Grace crying alone under the roots of a weeping tree. She woke one morning to seaweed curled around her ankles.

And then came the voice. A whisper in the wind:

"Go. Before the tide turns for good."

She knew what it meant.

She began preparing in secret. At night, she traced maps by oil lamp, memorizing departure schedules. She listened to dock workers from the shadows. She remembered every creak in the boards, every hidden nook her father had shown her. She used to play games with him, running barefoot along the hulls, hiding behind barrels.

But none of that mattered if she didn't solve two problems.

The first was Grace.

Could she bring her? Risk her life?

No.

Helen had seen enough mothers bury their young, and she refused to gamble Grace's breath on a chance.

So, she chose the only place left—her mother's home.

They hadn't spoken in years. Not since Helen accused her of poisoning her father with a curse. Her mother, a deeply spiritual woman who kept bones in her windows and salt at every doorframe, never denied the rumors.

"It was his time," she once said, her voice like cracked glass.

"Men who don't listen to the sea forget how to return."

Helen hated her for it.

But blood was blood. And Grace needed someone.

Her brother still lived there too, useless, drifting, always high on moon-smoke and muttering nonsense about forgotten gods. He had once tried to trade her wooden toys for dry herbs. She had never forgiven him.

Still, she wrapped Grace in Saint's old coat and kissed her forehead.

"You are my light," she whispered.

"I will come back with the storm," she said to herself.

She turned, knowing this would be the last night together, Grace falling asleep in her arms.

◆ ◆ ◆

Now, on the dock, she knelt by the water. She unwrapped a small bundle: salt, honey, rosemary, and a strand of Grace's hair. She dropped it into the tide.

"For safe passage," she said.

"And for return."

The sea carried it away.

Above her, the moon peeked through low clouds—waning, but not gone.

She stood, feeling something awaken in her bones.

TRE CHADO

It was time.

CHAPTER 2: THE PREPARATION

Helen stood beneath the low-hanging moon, a flickering lantern in one hand and another satchel in the other. The whisper of her sandals against the stone path was the only sound in the pre-dawn hush. The dock was no longer the only place where ghosts stirred.

She had made up her mind: she would sail west to find her husband and children. But to do so meant unraveling her last ties to this life. The first: her daughter, Grace.

No decision had ever torn her like this.

She looked down at the little girl beside her, barely past her tenth winter, with eyes too deep for her age and a mouth that rarely spoke unless she had something wise to say. Grace was silent now, her thin fingers gripping a bundle of sea-glass charms her father had once brought her.

Helen stopped walking. "I need to tell you something."

Grace looked up.

"I won't be here tomorrow."

Grace's lips pressed into a line. "I know," she said.

Helen knelt, brushing a curl from her daughter's face. "You're smart. Smarter than me sometimes. But you're still my child. And I need you to stay where you'll be safe."

"With Grandma?" Grace asked, with a sharpness that sliced Helen like coral.

"Yes," she said quietly.

Grace's brow furrowed. "She doesn't like you."

"She doesn't have to," Helen replied. "She just has to protect you."

The wind shifted. Somewhere beyond the hills, a night bird called twice. A bad omen, if you listened to the village women.

They approached the old homestead, half falling apart, shadowed by a crooked palm that had once been proud. The house smelled of lavender and mildew, its white paint now the color of sea foam. A single light flickered inside. A candle.

She's awake, Helen thought.

Her mother had always been strange. She spoke in riddles, lined her windows with feathers, and brewed teas that smelled like burned pine and sweet dirt. The village called her the Root-Mother. Some called her worse.

When Helen was younger, she remembered waking to the sound of her mother whispering prayers in a language not taught in school, something older, rawer, like wind moving through bones.

When her father died, Helen had stormed into the back room where her mother was grinding herbs into a blue clay bowl. "What did you do?" she screamed.

Her mother didn't flinch. "Only what the sea required."

Helen had never forgiven her.

But now, she stood at her door once more, holding the hand of her child, praying to the same spirits she once cursed.

The door creaked open.

Her mother stood there, tall and thin as reeds, with skin that looked carved from driftwood. Her gray eyes glinted in the candlelight.

"Helen," she said, as if they'd spoken yesterday.

"I need you to watch Grace."

Her mother looked down at the girl, then back at her daughter. "You always come home when the sea speaks."

"This time, I might not."

Her mother stepped aside. "Come in."

The inside hadn't changed, walls covered in dried herbs, jars filled with roots and ash, stones in spirals on the floor. Her brother, Abel, lounged on a cot in the corner, wrapped in a thick wool blanket, his eyes unfocused, lost in the sweet haze of moon-smoke.

"Still a ghost?" Helen muttered.

"He listens in ways others can't," her mother replied.

Grace clung closer.

Helen knelt before her daughter once more. "I'll be back, Grace. Or I won't. But you'll be alright. And you'll be strong."

Grace didn't cry. She handed her mother the sea-glass bundle. "For you. In case you forget me."

Helen took it, blinking hard. She kissed her daughter's forehead, then stood.

"I'm leaving before first bell," she told her mother.

"You always did run toward storms," the old woman said.

Outside, the wind had shifted again. Leaves whispered things they hadn't whispered in years.

◆ ◆ ◆

Back at her small home, Helen gathered the final pieces.

She had memorized the departure time of a merchant vessel carrying jade and silk to the west. It would leave in two days, and it was her only window.

But another problem pressed into her thoughts like a dull knife.

The tobacco ship.

She had heard it would arrive a week after the jade ship departed. Rumor held that it carried both goods and returning workers. Men with families, and sailors looking to reunite with the east.

What if Saint is on that ship? she thought. What if they are coming home, just as I'm leaving?

The weight of that possibility nearly undid her. She sat in the corner of her bedroom and rocked herself like she did in the weeks after Saint first left.

She lit a candle and whispered to it: If this is foolishness, take the wind from my sails. If it is truth, give me a sign.

The flame flickered. Then steadied.

A knock came at the door.

She rose, heart pounding. She opened it to find a cloaked woman with skin like ink and a smile that seemed to both soothe and pierce.

"I heard you were preparing to sail," she said.

"I might be," Helen replied.

"I'm Marlowe. I read tides. And I read dreams. Yours have been speaking."

Helen nodded slowly. She had heard of this woman, half healer, half wanderer. She came and went with the phases of the moon and claimed to speak for the water itself.

"I can tell you what I see," Marlowe said, stepping inside without invitation. "But only if you're ready."

Helen led her to the table.

Marlowe pulled out a stone, greenish-black, veined with white, and set it in a small bowl of saltwater.

She spoke words Helen didn't recognize.

Then silence.

Marlowe stared into the bowl.

"You are both the seeker and the storm," she said finally. "You leave now, or lose the tide forever. But know this, what you seek may not be what you find."

Helen felt her stomach twist.

"I need to know if my family is safe."

"They live," Marlowe said. "But they ache. And one watches the sea for your face."

"Which one?"

Marlowe smiled. "You'll know when you see them."

She stood and turned to leave. At the door, she added: "Do not travel during the bleeding moon. The sea forgets kindness during that phase."

Helen watched her vanish into the dark.

The wind whispered again.

She had two days.

CHAPTER 3: THE PLAN

The wind blew inland, as if trying to push her back. Helen stood in the shadows of the shipyard, hood pulled low, breath steady but hard. The salt in the air was thicker here, fermented with tar, sweat, and secrets. This was a place of uncertainty—certainly not for women.

But she wasn't a woman now.

She was no one. A name unspoken. A shape meant to blend with crates, ropes, and shadows. She had one goal: to board the jade ship before dawn two days from now.

The shipyard pulsed like a living thing—metal creaked, wooden wheels groaned, gulls screeched over half-unloaded goods. Every movement was ritual—sacred. Mistakes here meant not just injury, but curses, drowning, and death. Men tied red cords around their wrists to ward off "dock devils." No whistling was allowed, not even by wind. Whistling called storms, it was said—and storms remembered names.

Helen stayed low as she moved between the scaffolding and the crates, her eyes adjusting to the dark. The ship loomed ahead, a double-masted merchant vessel, its hull painted the color of old bones. Lanterns swung along its sides like fireflies preparing for war.

She knew this yard better than most of the men working it. Her father had once brought her here every Sunday at dawn, teaching her how to track footsteps in sawdust, how to hide from drunks, how to listen when no one thought you were there.

"Every ship speaks," he had told her once.

"But only children and fools hear it. Stay a child a little longer, Helen. Hear what they won't."

She had listened then. And she would listen now.

That night, she lit three candles in her small room and sat cross-legged on the floor with Saint's clothing laid before her like sacred relics.

She inhaled deeply, fingers trembling. A shirt. Trousers. A wool jacket patched at the elbows. She could smell him still—cedar, oil, and cinnamon from the bread he used to sneak from the dock kitchens.

Beside the clothes, she placed her hair, recently shorn, in a clay bowl. Then the sea-glass bundle Grace had given her. Then the salt.

One piece for love. One for blood. One for memory. One for protection.

She spoke a prayer, not one from her mother's book of herbs and whispers, but one she made up as a child with her father:

"Waves that guard, winds that carry, hide me as one, not many. Let the sea believe my face, and keep me walking in your grace."

She burned the hair and scattered the salt in a line across the floor.

Then she dressed.

She bound her chest tight with linen, pulled Saint's clothes over her skin, and tucked the glass bundle near her ribs where her heart beat loudest. She smeared a thin line of ash above her lip and pressed on the mustache she had carved from horsehair and pine resin.

When she looked in the cracked mirror, she didn't see a woman anymore.

She saw something in-between. Someone unfinished, unnamed. She saw survival.

At the shipyard, the days were long and the faces many. Helen spent the next morning watching the workers from behind a cracked storage crate, studying their rhythms.

That's when she noticed him.

A man in his early twenties, tall with heavy eyes and a crooked smile. His shirt clung to his back with sweat, and he moved like someone who didn't want to be seen, but wanted to be watched. She recognized that kind of stillness, too practiced.

He caught her gaze.

"You're not one of them," he said, with a voice like gravel softened by wine.

She tensed. He took a step closer.

"Don't worry. I remember you."

Her heart dropped. She looked away.

"Baron," he said with a bow that mocked grace.

"From the village, remember? I was at your father's funeral. I brought the black orchids."

A chill ran down her spine. She remembered those orchids. They had appeared on her windowsill days after the burial, no note, just dark petals with a scent like burnt clove. She had never asked where they came from.

"I used to watch you," Baron continued.

"When you ran along the docks as a child. Always barefoot. Always angry. I thought you were beautiful even then."

Helen's fingers curled into fists.

"I'm just trying to help," he said, more softly now.

"If anyone asks, you're my cousin from Hollow Bend. Keep close to me. I'll get you on that ship."

She said nothing, but nodded.

Over the next two days, Baron kept close. Too close. He directed her—where to lift crates, when to hide, when to breathe. At night, he found excuses to linger nearby. Once, she woke to find him standing by her makeshift cot, staring at her with something between longing and possession.

"You could stay," he whispered.

"You don't need to find him. I'm here."

She turned her back to him.

The next morning, she moved alone.

The yard was restless. A sailor slipped and cracked his skull, the third time in two days. Someone spotted a shark circling too close to the pier. Others swore they heard singing from beneath the waves.

"Something cursed is near," they muttered.

"The sea smells off."

Helen kept moving. She had no time for omens, only the plan.

She stole rations when she could. Bits of dried fish, crusts of bread, and a flask of brine-thick water. She learned to keep her gaze low, shoulders hunched, voice gruff. Every movement had to be calculated. Each misstep could mean discovery and death.

She spent one night hiding in a fishing skiff abandoned along the dock's end. There, beneath an old tarp, she etched a map into the wood: ship routes, guard shifts, a small sketch of the jade ship's frame.

Her father had once taught her how to memorize maps by touch. Eyes closed, fingers following grain, she learned each pathway until it felt like muscle memory.

The last night on the docks, she heard footsteps approaching her makeshift hideout. She held her breath, clutching a wooden handle like a dagger.

"Don't be scared," Baron's voice called.

"I brought you something."

He dropped a bundle: a tattered wool cloak, warm and dry. Helen took it with numb hands.

"Thank you," she said, almost meaning it.

He lingered. "You don't belong in the west, you know. You're made for deeper things."

She didn't respond. Eventually, he walked away.

◆ ◆ ◆

On the night before departure, Helen crept to the edge of the shipyard and lit a candle for her children. She spoke each of their names, tracing them with ash along the railing: Grace, Light, Tempest, Storm.

Then she added her father's name—and Saint's.

She watched the flame sputter and go out.

She did not cry.

◆ ◆ ◆

On the final morning, she dressed in full disguise— bound her chest, tucked her hair, and recited her prayer. She stepped out into the mist with the tide rising behind her.

Baron was waiting.

"You sure you want this?" he asked.

"Yes," she said simply.

"Then let's get you aboard."

The horn blew. The ship's belly opened. She stepped into the unknown, knowing only this: her path was her own. And not even love—especially the twisted kind—could deter her now.

CHAPTER 4: OH NO

Six weeks into the voyage, the sea was no longer romantic. It was relentless.

Waves pounded the hull like fists from an angry god, while winds screamed through the rigging, lashing the crew into shadows of themselves. Helen kept to her post near the lower deck, stacking crates, mending rope, and avoiding eye contact. She didn't speak unless spoken to. She became a whisper. A shadow.

Baron hovered.

He watched her with eyes too soft and too sharp. At night, when the crew slept below deck in swaying hammocks, he sat near her feet, chewing on bits of seaweed and telling stories she didn't ask for. When he touched her arm, she would jerk away and pretend it was the rocking of the ship.

"I heard once," he said one night, "that if a woman boards a ship without being welcomed by the tide, the sea curses her with a voice the wind can hear, but no one else can."

Helen said nothing. She adjusted her bandages, pretending not to flinch.

"I'd know if someone was cursed," he added.

"I'd feel it."

His tone made her stomach twist. Sometimes she thought he was watching not to protect her, but to possess her.

◆ ◆ ◆

Storms worsened.

The crew muttered about omens. Someone found a dying seagull tangled in the rigging. A barrel of fish went sour overnight. Knots came undone without being touched. And worst of all, iron tools began to rust and turn cold—even near the cook fires.

"That ain't normal," grunted one sailor.

"Something's on this ship that shouldn't be."

Another spat overboard.

"We're carrying silk and jade. Maybe the gods don't like what we're trading."

"No," said the shipwright, a man whose arms were as thick as driftwood.

"It's a woman. I can feel it. A woman's aboard. The sea don't take kindly to liars wearing boots."

Helen's breath caught.

Baron stood nearby, leaning against a post, hands folded, an unreadable expression shadowing his face.

◆ ◆ ◆

The crew grew restless. Suspicion thickened like mist. Superstitions became law.

The navigator lost his sense of direction for three straight days. The captain blamed the stars, but no one believed it. Some whispered that songs had been heard below deck—soft lullabies in a voice no one recognized.

They stopped whistling entirely. Even the wind seemed to hold its breath.

That night, Helen returned to her sleeping spot only to find it soaked in seawater. A strange symbol had been scratched into the wood beside it—a spiral crossed by three vertical lines.

She recognized it from her mother's books.

A mark of exposure—the sign given when a hidden truth had been noticed by the spirits.

She looked up and saw Baron watching her from across the deck. Smiling. A smile that held no warmth.

◆ ◆ ◆

Then came the stillness.

The next morning, the sea was motionless. A glassy pane reflecting gray skies and dread.

No wind. No waves. Just silence.

It was worse than the storms.

The captain ordered every man topside.

"We've angered something," he said, his voice low but firm.

"We will find it, face it, and feed it to the sea until it's satisfied."

They began to search. Cargo was pried open. Hammocks stripped. Boots inspected. Torsos exposed for hidden marks.

Helen retreated to the captain's quarters under the guise of cleaning. She scrubbed the floor with trembling hands, trying to steady her breath.

That's when the door creaked open.

Baron entered.

He closed the door behind him and leaned against it.

"They're going to find you," he said.

She stood, eyes burning.

"You don't belong here," he added.

"You never did. And he won't want you. Not after all this."

She took a step back. "Baron, don't..."

"I could help you," he said, his voice laced with desperation.

"If you just... if you stayed with me. If you stopped chasing ghosts."

Helen's pulse roared in her ears. "My family aren't ghost."

Baron's expression twisted. "Then drown with them."

He turned, yanked the door open, and shouted down the hall.

"I found her!"

The crew stormed the quarters.

Hands grabbed her arms. Someone tore the jacket from her back. Her disguise unraveled beneath their fists—linen bindings, the ash mustache, the illusion of manhood—all stripped like lies in the wind.

Gasps rose. A sailor crossed himself. One man cried out and fell to his knees.

The captain stood before her, face pale, his voice shaking not from fear, but fury.

"Do you know what you've done?" he asked.

Helen met his gaze.

"I did what I had to."

He stepped forward, his breath sour with rum and rage.

"You brought disease, confusion, and ruin. This ship has been cursed since port because of you."

"It was cursed long before I came aboard," she said through gritted teeth.

Someone struck her.

Baron watched silently, eyes vacant, as if he were somewhere far away.

They dragged her to the center of the deck. The sky boiled above, clouds coiling like serpents. The air was still.

The captain addressed the crew.

"This woman lied. Hid among us like a snake in the bilge. She cursed this ship with her deceit. She ignored every sacred rule of the sea."

Some men wept. Others muttered prayers. One whispered,

"We should burn her."

But the captain raised a hand. "The sea will judge. We will bind her. Strip her. Mark her. And give her back to the tide."

Baron turned away as they tore her clothes. She stood naked before the crew, back straight, tears silent. Not for shame, but for rage.

"I came for love," Helen said.

"No," the captain spat. "You came for mutiny."

They bound her wrists with rough rope and carved a symbol into her shoulder—a jagged spiral matching the one near her bunk. It bled, slow and steady. The pain was nothing compared to the fire inside her.

One of the older sailors stepped forward, his voice shaking. "We can't… this isn't right."

"She broke the sea's law," the captain said.

"And we'll all suffer if we do nothing."

The sailor stepped back. No one else spoke.

At dusk, they brought her to the plank.

The sea waited, quiet and dark.

The shipwright tied a cannonball to her ankle. "So you sink, not swim," he muttered.

She looked up at the sky. No birds. No stars. Only gray.

She thought of Grace. Of Saint. Of her children's laughter echoing down quiet halls.

She whispered the lullaby her father once sang:

"O sea, O sea, return to me, what time and tide have stole. O moon, O moon, remember soon, the cost of seeking whole."

Then she stepped forward on her own, walking not in defeat but defiance.

And the sea swallowed her.

CHAPTER 5: DEATH

The water hit her like silence. Not the kind that soothes. The kind that reminds you no one is coming.

As the sea accepted her, Helen didn't struggle. She didn't flail or scream. She let the cold wrap around her like an old shawl, familiar and absolute. The cannonball tied to her ankle dragged her steadily downward, pulling her out of the fading light and into a world without color.

The sea closed above her like a second sky. The ship vanished. The judgmental faces blurred. Even Baron's betrayal—if you could call it that—dissolved like salt.

What remained was the sound of her heartbeat and the slow, painful creaking of her bones under pressure.

This is what the end feels like, she thought.

But it wasn't terror that filled her.

It was remembering.

◆ ◆ ◆

First came the children.

Their faces appeared in the bubbles around her, each one framed by soft golden light. Grace, calm and composed, clutching her sea-glass charms. Light, with his crooked grin. Tempest, singing nonsense rhymes. And Storm, still chubby-cheeked and curious, pointing up at the stars.

They didn't speak. But their eyes did.

Not "goodbye."

Not even "come back."

Only "remember."

◆ ◆ ◆

The deeper she sank, the more time unraveled.

She saw Saint on their wedding day, his eyes bright beneath the moon. He held her hands, wrapped in the rigger's rope. His lips moved, whispering promises.

Then, the scene blurred.

He was on the dock, waiting. But he wasn't waiting for her. He looked older. Tired. A girl stood beside him with Grace's eyes and Helen's hair.

They turned away.

She reached for them, but her arms no longer obeyed.

◆ ◆ ◆

The pressure grew.

As her chest collapsed, the water squeezed against her skin like invisible hands, trying to mold her into something else.

Then, a glow.

Below her, far beneath the reach of sun or moon, something stirred.

Shapes. Not quite human. Not quite fish.

A song began—low, vibrating through her bones before reaching her ears.

It was the same lullaby her father used to hum. But it was older now. Wiser—like it had grown teeth.

"O sea, O sea, remember me, the child of shore and grief. O womb, O tomb, undo this doom, and judge my soul beneath."

She opened her eyes fully, and there before her was a woman made of water.

Skin like shifting tides. Hair like the color of sea at its deepest hour in motion. Eyes hollow but knowing. Her arms stretched wide.

Helen's breath left her.

Not from drowning. From awe.

"Are you death?" she asked, or thought she did.

The sea-woman smiled.

"No," came the voice.

"I am memory. I am trial. I am the gate you chose."

The water grew warm around Helen, like an embrace. Her body no longer burned. Her lungs no longer begged.

"I came for love," she whispered.

The sea-woman tilted her head. "You came for longing. That is not the same."

"I came for my children."

"No. You came because you could no longer bear thinking that you have been left behind."

Tears rose in Helen's eyes. But they didn't float away. They became pearls.

The sea-woman lifted one.

"You carry shame, rage, and sacrifice. But you left no room for surrender."

"What do you want from me?"

"To choose."

◆ ◆ ◆

The water changed.

Suddenly, Helen stood on the dock again.

But everything was different. The sky was black. The moon had cracked in two. The village burned in the distance. Fish flopped on the sand, gasping for air.

Saint stood nearby, but his eyes were empty. Grace sat in the boat, humming a twisted version of the lullaby. A shadow with Baron's voice whispered from behind her,

"You could've stayed. You could've stayed."

"No!" Helen screamed.

The dock gave way beneath her.

She was falling again.

◆ ◆ ◆

This time, she landed not in water, but in her mother's old herb room.

Smoke filled the air. The walls whispered names.

A bowl of ashes sat in front of her.

"Burn your name," her mother's voice said.

"Or keep carrying the weight."

She hesitated. Then reached into the bowl.

Her own name burned in red letters: Helen.

She touched it, and fire spread through her body.

Pain surged. But beneath it, clarity.

She screamed—not in pain, in conviction.

The smoke dissolved.

She was back underwater.

The sea-woman waited.

"You are no longer who you were," she said.

Helen looked down at her hands.

The rope-burns were gone. Her scars faded. Her body felt lighter —not because the cannonball had been removed, but because she had let go.

"Do you wish to live?" the sea-woman asked.

"I wish to become."

"Then rise."

◆ ◆ ◆

The cannonball broke.

Not with force—with liberation.

It fell into the depths like a dropped memory, forgotten and weightless.

Helen rose slowly, carried not by her limbs, but by the breath she thought she had lost.

Above her, the sea opened—like a rebirth.

She broke the surface, gasping.

But there was no ship.

Only horizon.

Only sky.

And in the distance, a voice. A child's voice.

"Mommy?"

Helen turned toward the sound.

She began to swim.

Each stroke came not from muscle, but from will.

The tide didn't fight her. It lifted her.

In the sky above, gulls returned. A sunbeam slipped through the clouds.

Somewhere on another ship, a sailor sat upright in his hammock, clutching his chest.

"I just saw a ghost," he whispered.

But Helen was no ghost.

She was something the sea had remade.

And she was not finished yet.

CHAPTER 6: SAINT

The ship docked just after first light, its hull scraping the pier like a tired sigh. The crew stretched, shouted greetings, and unloaded their freight: tobacco bundles wrapped in tar-stained canvas, crates of salted meats, and hand-bound scrolls marked with red wax.

But Saint wasn't looking at the cargo.

He was looking for her.

He stood on the deck with his children gathered around him—his frame hardened by two years of labor, his face shaded by a beard that hadn't been there when he left. As the mist burned away, he stepped onto solid ground and whispered, "I'm back, Helen."

No answer. No figure waiting on the dock. No candle in the distance.

His heart thudded once, then once more.

"Papa," Storm said, pulling on his sleeve.

"Are we home?"

"Almost," he said, forcing a smile.

He looked at her closely. Storm was taller now. Her eyes sharper, her voice steadier. She looked too much like her mother in the early mornings, when the world was still quiet and full of questions.

Saint gathered his bags. Light ran ahead, racing a seagull. Tempest hummed a tune Helen used to sing. Storm began walking steadily, looking over her shoulder as if someone had followed them.

Saint paused. The wind carried a strange scent—salt, sure, but something else.

Smoked lavender. His wife's scent.

◆ ◆ ◆

Saint had made a deal with the tobacco company two years earlier. It was not a deal made lightly.

He remembered the day clearly. The foreman had pulled him aside into his office after a long shift.

"You want to go back East?" the man asked, after sitting down, his eyes fixed on the ledger.

"Take your children?"

"Yes," Saint replied.

"One year contract. You carry what we give you, don't ask questions, and return with everything intact. You'll get passage. No more, no less."

Saint had nodded. He had no choice.

The West was cruel in its offerings. Food was scarce, prejudice plentiful, and work always one wrong word from collapse. But he had kept his head down. Carried the crates. Packaged what was sometimes tobacco, sometimes something else. He asked no questions.

For his children.

He remembered nights when Storm cried for her mother. When Tempest asked if they'd been abandoned. When Light sat silently on the edge of his cot, watching the stars, wishing they might answer.

He had held them all and promised, "We will go home. I'll bring you back."

He had wanted to return sooner. One year in, he had begged the company to let him leave.

"My wife is waiting," he had said. "I have to go back."

They refused. "You're too good at what you do."

He clenched his jaw and packed the next crate with trembling hands.

The children saw more than he thought they would. Storm caught him crying in the storage room one night. He'd told her the salt in his eyes was from the sea air. She didn't believe him.

◆ ◆ ◆

Now, back in the East, the children ran ahead toward the dock's end. Saint looked around. The town looked the same—weathered signs, slow-moving boats, villagers too tired to speak.

But the dock was empty.

She should be here.

He tried to convince himself she was simply late. Maybe she was ill. Maybe she didn't know he was coming. Maybe...

He shook his head. No. She would know.

He made his way toward the village. Storm trailed beside him, glancing sideways.

"Papa... where's Mama?"

He didn't answer.

He stopped at an old vendor first. The man recognized him and nodded.

"Back from the dead?"

"Looking for Helen."

The man's expression changed. "You better talk to Fish."

That name burned like cold metal.

Fish had always been loyal, to a fault. He had helped Helen when Saint left, watched her closely, and longed for her peace. Saint remembered once finding a red string tied to their front door. A ward. Helen had claimed Fish put it there for safety.

Saint had never trusted it.

He found Fish behind the warehouse, skin still burned bronze from the sun, still carrying the same long pipe carved from bone.

Fish squinted. "Didn't expect to see you again."

Saint nodded. "Where is she?"

Fish sucked on the pipe for a long moment before answering.

"She asked for help a couple moons ago. She wanted to get on the jade ship."

Saint's heart sank.

"You let her go?"

"I told her no."

Saint's chest lifted with hope.

Fish shook his head. "But she got on anyway."

Saint took a step forward. "How?"

"She disguised herself. Used your old clothes. Said she was going west to find her family."

Silence passed between them like thunder on the horizon.

"She left Grace with her mother," Fish added.

"Didn't say goodbye to anyone else."

Saint exhaled hard, a mix of grief and guilt slamming into his ribs.

"And you let her go?"

Fish shrugged. "She wasn't mine to stop."

Saint clenched his fists. He wanted to scream. Wanted to shake the man. But what good would it do?

He looked out toward the sea.

"I'm going to get her."

Fish tilted his head. "She might already be lost."

"She's not."

◆ ◆ ◆

Saint gathered the children and made his way toward Helen's mother's house.

He hadn't stepped foot near that place in years. He hated it. Not for what it was, but for what it reminded him of. The root work. The whispered spells. The night he saw Helen standing barefoot in a salt circle, crying without sound.

He remembered her saying, "She doesn't love people. She binds them. That's different."

He knocked once.

The door creaked open.

Light darted in first, calling for his grandmother. Tempest followed, but Storm clung to Saint's leg.

Then the witch appeared.

She hadn't changed. Still tall and thin, wrapped in a robe that smelled of iron and herbs. Her eyes were too clear—too knowing.

"I see the prodigal son has returned," she said.

"I'm not here for games."

"No," she said. "You're here for truth."

Saint stepped inside. The house hummed. Something unseen shifted in the shadows.

He asked for Grace. She was in the back, feeding chickens. When she came inside and saw him, she dropped the feed bucket and ran into his arms.

"You came back," she whispered.

"I told you I would."

The reunion was short-lived.

The witch poured tea and told him what he didn't want to hear.

"She went west. Disguised. Took your scent with her. I warned her. The sea doesn't forgive lies."

"Did she return?" Saint asked.

"She hasn't. Not in body."

The room darkened. The air thickened.

"But she walks the tides now," the witch added. "Not all who drown are gone. Some just learn to breathe differently."

Out of frustration and anger, Saint left without saying a word.

That night, Saint couldn't sleep.

He lay beside Grace, listening to the wind. The children murmured in their sleep. The waves crashed louder than usual.

At one point, he stood and went outside.

The moon hung high, waxing, nearly full.

He looked to the sea.

For a moment—just one heartbeat—he saw her.

A figure in the water. Hair floating like seaweed. Arms open.

Then gone.

He whispered, "Helen."

The wind answered with a lullaby.

CHAPTER 7:
WITCH IN LAW

Saint went back the next day and stood at the edge of the garden, staring at the crooked palm tree that marked the entrance to his past.

The goat tied beneath it stared back, chewing calmly as if it had all the time in the world.

This was the same tree where Helen's father used to sit after long days at sea, Bible in hand, boots muddy, eyes sharp. The same tree where he'd once told Saint, "You will be the unraveling of this family."

And still, Saint had married her.

Not out of lust. Out of love.

But it was her mother he had never trusted. Even in silence, she was too loud. In her presence, everything felt watched. She made tea that simmered without fire. Herbs hung from her ceilings in shapes he didn't understand. And every child who entered the house seemed to leave changed.

He remembered how Helen used to call her the Witch-In-Law, joking lightly but with a tremble beneath her laughter. She claimed her mother kept jars of tears under the floorboards, though Saint had never checked.

Now, here he was again. With four children and a wound he didn't yet have a name for.

◆ ◆ ◆

He knocked.

The door creaked open slowly, and there stood Abel, Helen's brother pale, sunken-eyed, and shirtless. His pupils were dilated. A faint line of powder rimmed his nostrils.

Saint stiffened.

"Where are the children?" he asked.

Abel shrugged. "They are around back with the chickens."

Even though Saint had a problem with Helen's mother, he never restricted the children from her, even with his difference of opinion.

Saint stepped forward. Abel didn't move. Saint pushed past him.

The house smelled of salt, smoke, rosemary, and something like bloodroot. The air wasn't compressed—it was thick, like it had its own body. Jars lined every wall, each filled with dark liquid or dried plants. Some had things floating inside that he didn't want to look at twice. He passed a mirror that seemed to darken when he glanced at it.

Then she appeared again.

Helen's mother.

She walked in barefoot, her feet covered in ash. Her robe trailed behind her like smoke. Her eyes, pale as bone, locked onto his. She felt different since he last saw her. Her hair fell down her back—midnight, streaked silver, threaded with beads carved from bone and shell.

"Well, well," she said. "The wind has returned one of its missing things."

She said it like it was the first time she had seen him since he'd been back.

Saint clenched his jaw. "Where are my children?"

"They are safe."

"And my wife?"

She poured tea.

"As I told you yesterday, she's been given to the sea."

Saint stepped forward. "What do you mean—given?"

"She chose it. The sea doesn't take unless it's summoned."

He slammed a hand on the table. "You knew. You always knew she would go."

"I warned her. She carried too much grief. It bends people toward the water."

"She didn't drown."

"No," the witch said. "She changed."

She turned her back on him and began stirring the tea with a feather. The cup glowed briefly, then dimmed.

◆ ◆ ◆

Grace entered the room, feathers in her hair and dirt on her hands. She smiled when she saw him.

"Papa."

He knelt and wrapped her in his arms, but her small body felt... different.

Not colder. Not warmer.

Just older.

She pulled back. "I dreamt of her."

"Your mother?" Grace nodded. "She was underwater. But not sad."

"What did she say?"

"She sang. And she said not to be afraid of the dark parts."

Saint's breath caught. That was something Helen used to whisper to her when Grace was small and frightened by storms.

That night, Saint stayed at the house.

He didn't want to, but the storm had rolled in suddenly, and the children were tired.

The air inside the home shifted as soon as the sun set.

The lamps flickered.

The house creaked in rhythms too precise to be random.

The witch moved from room to room, barefoot and humming. Abel disappeared into the attic.

Saint tried to sleep on the old couch, but the dreams came quickly.

In them, Helen stood at the dock, soaked to the bone. Her lips were blue, but she smiled. She held something out to him—a bundle wrapped in seaweed.

When he opened it, it was his own heart, still beating.

He woke in a sweat, the scent of the ocean lingering in his nose.

In the morning, he found Grace kneeling in front of the old hearth.

"What are you doing?" he asked.

"I'm listening," she said.

"To what?"

"To Mama. She sings through the fire now."

Saint knelt beside her. "Baby, that's not possible."

Grace turned. "Didn't you say nothing's impossible for love?"

He was silent.

Then Abel stumbled downstairs, half-dressed, eyes wide.

"She spoke to me," he whispered. "In the wall. She said not to let them leave."

Saint rose. "What?"

The witch entered the room, calm as always. "They're waking to her."

Saint stepped between the witch and his children. "You're not going to put your madness in their heads."

"I don't have to," she said. "She's already in them."

Grace stood and walked to the palm tree. She began tying a red cord around its trunk, just like the ones the sailors wore.

Saint watched, mouth dry.

"She said the sea remembers," Grace whispered. "And it's waiting."

That afternoon, the wind died completely.

Even the chickens were quiet. Abel stayed curled in his cot, muttering the names of ancient gods that had not been spoken in generations.

The witch began to prepare herbs and stones, placing them in a bag made from sealskin.

"You'll need this if you want to reach her," she said.

Saint frowned. "What do you mean?"

"She's not just across the sea. She's beyond it now. If you go without protection, you'll drown, not in water—but in memory."

Saint took the bag reluctantly. Inside were obsidian shards, lavender, a conch shell, and a slip of parchment with a symbol he couldn't decipher.

He looked to Grace, who was drawing a spiral in the dirt.

"Are you ready?" he asked.

She nodded.

Tempest and Storm stood behind her, holding hands.

Light walked up beside Saint. "We all are."

That night, as the tide rose again and the moon hung high, Saint turned to the sea.

"I'm coming, Helen."

And the wind, at last, replied: Hurry.

CHAPTER 8: ON
MY WAY

The wind had shifted again. It carried not the scent of salt or rain, but memory, smoke from old fires, songs once sung by lips now silenced, and the ache of names whispered across water.

Saint stood at the edge of the dock, his children beside him. Grace clutched a red cord in one hand. Storm wore her mother's old scarf. Light held the small wooden knife Saint had carved during their first year out west. And Tempest? He said nothing. He only watched the sea like it owed him something.

They waited for the captain.

Saint had spoken to him the night before—a man with steel-gray hair and a gold ring through his eyebrow, who didn't ask why Saint needed to return west so soon.

"You look like a man chasing a ghost," the captain had said.

Saint didn't reply.

As they waited, Grace leaned against her father's leg.

"Will she know we're coming?"

Saint looked down. "She already knows."

"How?"

"She's your mother. She always knew before we did."

Grace nodded, as if that explained everything.

They boarded the tobacco ship at sunrise.

The new crew was quiet. Tired. Many of them looked at Saint with a strange sort of recognition, as though they'd seen him in a dream.

The ship groaned as it pulled from shore, leaving behind a village that no longer felt like home.

◆ ◆ ◆

The journey began.

The sea stretched endlessly ahead.

By the fifth day, the rhythm of ship life settled in: meals, watch, and prayer. But unease lurked beneath the order.

Saint noticed it first—strange whispers from the lower deck, tools missing, then reappearing in odd places. Tempest complained of someone humming under the floorboards. Storm said her shoes were wet when she woke.

At first, Saint thought the children were playing into the sailors' fears.

Then the cook's assistant vanished.

They found his knife near the storage crates, freshly used, no blood in sight.

On the seventh day, the captain summoned Saint at dawn.

"Come with me," he said, his face pale.

They descended into the dark hold of the ship, past hanging ropes and swaying lanterns, until they reached the rear cargo bay.

Saint smelled salt—and something fouler.

The crew stood in a tight circle, backs rigid.

At the center, curled like a snake behind stacked barrels, was a man.

His lips moved without sound. His eyes were wide, red-rimmed, and unfocused. He rocked slightly, cradling something in his arms.

It was a handful of red cord, knotted over and over again.

Saint stepped closer.

The man looked up.

Baron.

He was sunburnt and half-starved. His clothes were soaked with brine. Symbols were scratched into the wooden floor around him —swirls, hooks, and spirals.

"She sang to me..." Baron rasped. "She opened her arms..."

Saint's chest tightened.

The captain spat. "A stowaway."

"He's cursed," muttered a sailor.

"No," Saint said. "He's worse. He's obsessed."

The captain turned to Saint. "He's yours to deal with. What do you want done?"

Saint looked into Baron's glazed-over eyes. Something deep and wrong moved behind them. The way he clutched the red cord— like a holy relic.

"Chain him," Saint said. "And keep him away from the children."

The sailors hesitated, then dragged Baron out of the circle. He screamed at first, then laughed.

"She's waiting for us all," he whispered. "And she's not alone anymore."

◆ ◆ ◆

After Baron's capture, the ship entered a stretch of sea no one recognized. It wasn't marked on maps. The water shimmered violet at dawn and turned black as obsidian by dusk. Birds refused to follow. Even the stars looked wrong.

Storm began to sing in her sleep. Grace's eyes glowed faintly under the moonlight. Light carved the same spiral over and over into the ship's railing.

Tempest refused to speak. He only stared at the waves.

One night, Saint woke to the sound of humming. He followed it to the upper deck, where Grace stood alone, arms outstretched to the horizon.

"Go back to bed," he said gently.

"She's almost here," Grace whispered.

Saint looked out.

There, standing on the water, was Helen.

Helen's figure did not move. Her hair swirled around her as if stirred by unseen tides. Her eyes glowed softly, not white, not gold, but the deep blue of the ocean's oldest trench.

She raised a hand.

The ship's bell rang on its own.

Below deck, Baron began to scream. Chains rattled. Wood splintered. Then silence.

Saint turned. The hatch to the hold swung open. Baron climbed out slowly, like a marionette pulled by invisible strings.

He looked different. Taller. Boneless.

"Forgive me," he whispered to the children, and leapt overboard.

Not a splash. Just absorption.

The crew gathered. Some prayed. Others wept.

Saint walked to the rail.

He met Helen's gaze.

She said nothing. But he heard her.

"Bring them."

He turned to his children.

"This is the moment. If you're afraid, stay. If you believe, follow."

They stepped forward.

Together, they climbed the rail.

With one last breath, they stepped into the sea.

CHAPTER 9:
TOGETHER FOR NEVER

The sea accepted them with silence. Saint and his children stepped off the ship and onto the surface of the water, not swimming, not sinking, but walking, as if memory itself had hardened into a path.

Helen stood just ahead. She didn't move, but her presence pulled them forward. Her gown shimmered like a tide under moonlight, layered with strands of kelp and woven coral. Her eyes were vast and voidless. They no longer held just the woman Saint had married—they held the memory of tsunamis, the ache of drowned lullabies, the hush of deep trenches.

Grace reached her first.

"Mommy," she whispered.

Her voice broke with wonder, not sorrow.

Helen knelt and wrapped her daughter in her arms. Her body was cold, yet comforting. Like a wave that had waited too long.

One by one, the children embraced her. Tempest. Light. Storm. When Saint came last, Helen looked up with a half-smile that crumbled every wall he had built inside.

He knelt beside her, placing his forehead to hers.

"I'm sorry," he whispered.

"I was never lost," she replied. "Only waiting."

◆ ◆ ◆

The water began to glow.

Around them, the sea shifted, forming a circle of light. From the depths rose shapes, not fully human, not fully spirit. The guardians of the deep. Sirens who had learned silence. Mermaids with songs bound in braids. Drowned men who had forgotten their names.

They surrounded the family—not with menace, but with reverence.

This was a ceremony.

A reunion.

The sea was not taking them.

It was receiving them.

Helen rose, now fully aglow. She held a conch shell in one hand. From it emerged a low hum—the sound that had haunted the ship's crew, that had drawn Baron to madness, that had lulled her children in dreams.

The Song of the Deep.

It was not a song of death.

It was a song of return.

Saint and the children joined in, not with words, but breath. Together, they drifted lower into the sea—embraced by its rhythm.

They did not drown.

They transformed.

Their feet melted into fin and memory. Their lungs adjusted to the tides. Their eyes learned the language of fish and current.

Helen kissed each of them, sealing the bond.

"We are no longer of land," she said. "We are story now."

The sea began to shift again, and as it did, visions unfolded on its surface like paintings come to life.

They saw the past: Helen kneeling on the dock, binding her chest with linen and whispering prayers to the moon. Saint carving wooden animals to calm Light. Grace being born beneath the gaze of her grandmother, her first cry cutting through a rainstorm. All those moments once thought lost, now preserved in salt and sea.

Then came the deeper memories. Those not of their family, but of the sea itself. The birth of the first wave. The death of the first sailor. The voice of the first mother who whispered her child's name into the ocean, never to hear it echoed back.

"We remember everything," said one of the sirens. Her voice was fluid—without a single break in breath. "The sea is not only water. It is memory. It is judgment. It is mercy."

Helen stepped forward, her gown trailing stars. She turned to Saint.

"Do you still fear me?" she asked.

"I fear forgetting you," he replied.

"Then come deeper."

◆ ◆ ◆

They followed her into the deeper dark. Down into canyons of silence where ships lay cracked and open like forgotten letters. They swam past jellyfish with bells of lightning, past skeletons of leviathans so massive they could have swallowed cities.

There, in the pressure where only faith could breathe, was a temple carved into black coral.

It pulsed with song.

Inside, other souls waited. Not all were human. Some were bird-boned. Others plant-veined. They had once loved, and once lost, and now held space for the next tide.

Helen placed her hand on the temple gate. It opened like a sigh.

◆ ◆ ◆

Within the temple, Grace was shown a pool.

In it, she saw herself, not now, but older. Wiser. Standing before a crowd. Speaking in a voice that echoed like bells wrapped in water.

"You will lead," the sea-mother said. "When the tide rises again."

Storm was gifted a shell. Inside, a voice sang each night, teaching her how to bend wind and current. Light was taught how to heal with water. Tempest, silent, had always known how to speak to the sea.

Saint was given a memory, the day Helen chose the sea over silence. He watched her pain, her strength, her longing. And he forgave it all.

He forgave himself.

◆ ◆ ◆

Back on the ship, the crew sat in stunned stillness.

No one spoke. The captain wept quietly.

The sea, which had been so cruel, was now still. Not empty. Just patient.

They heard the lullaby again, faint, then fading.

When the ship returned to port, only Grace stood on deck.

But she wasn't only Grace anymore.

She stepped off barefoot, hair wet, eyes like glass polished by centuries.

Fish was there, waiting.

"You came back," he said, eyes wide.

"I came to begin again," Grace replied.

She walked past him and toward the mountain.

In the village, people changed.

Children began humming lullabies they didn't know.

Sailors refused to whistle.

Fishermen began tying red cords to their ankles, not their wrists.

They said the sea had softened.

They said something sacred had been returned to it.

And at the edge of the dock, just beyond where the palm trees swayed, a girl with black-ice hair often stood, watching the tide.

She would stay there for hours.

Not waiting.

Just listening.

To the waves.

To the stories.

To the promise that always meant forever.

And that love, once offered to the sea, always returned in a new form.

Helen of the West.

The tide turns.

The next current begins.